This book belongs to:

For the crew at Fairhaven School – A.B.

For my mum, who paints the ocean,
and my dad, who makes our craft – D.T.

PUFFIN

UK | USA | Canada | Ireland | Australia
India | New Zealand | South Africa | China

Puffin is an imprint of the Penguin Random House group of companies, whose addresses can be found at global.penguinrandomhouse.com.

First published by Penguin Random House New Zealand, 2020

3 5 7 9 10 8 6 4

Design by Cat Taylor © Penguin Random House New Zealand
Prepress by Image Centre Group
Printed and bound in China by Asia Pacific Offset Limited

A catalogue record for this book is available from the National Library of New Zealand.

ISBN 978-0-14-377429-7

penguin.co.nz

THE BOYS IN THE WAKA AMA

PUFFIN

WRITTEN BY
Angie Belcher

ILLUSTRATED BY
Debbie Tipuna

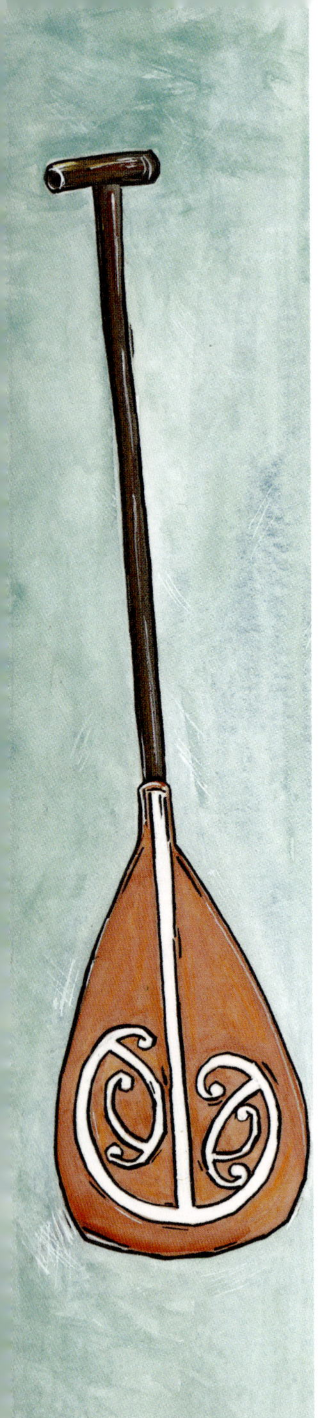

Tahi, rua, toru, whā!

Hoe! Hoe! Hoe!

These are the boys

who paddle the **waka ama**.

IRIRANGI
NIXON
WILL
IOSEFA
ZAC
NIKO

This is the **waka**, alone in the shed,

that waits for the boys to get out of bed.

It's bathed in the light from the sun at dawn,

which wakes the boys, who stretch and yawn,

before paddling the **waka ama**.

TIPUNA TYR

These are the boys, determined and strong,

who carry the **waka** and chant a song.

They check the flotations are carefully stashed

and the ropes on the crossbeams are carefully lashed,

before paddling the **waka ama**.

NGĀ WAKA E WHITU
E TAU NEI
HOEA HOEA RĀ

They gather together for **karakia**,

a quiet moment, a thoughtful prayer,

to acknowledge the power of the wind and the sea,

and guide them and their waka safely,

before paddling the **waka ama**.

This is the **kaihautū**, who watches the sea
and guides the waka to where it should be.
He leads the boys, so determined and strong,
who paddle the waka and chant a song.
They pick up their paddles, which dip and row,
and make the waka go fast and flow
across the sea, so calm and smooth,
which ripples and glints as the waka moves,
as they paddle the **waka ama**.

KAIHOE.
HOEA TŌ WAKA

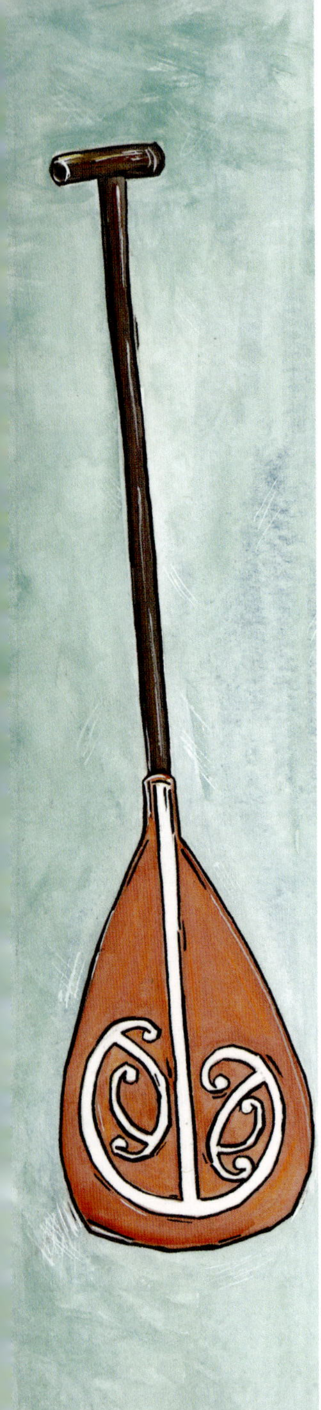

These are the crews of the **waka**, which race

side-by-side at a heart-thumping pace.

It's a white-water frenzy, there's nothing between

the waka, which race as a closely knit team.

Their **whānau** have gathered along the shore —

"**Kia tere! Kia tere! Kia tere** — give more!"

The waka glides faster, the boys dig in deep.

There will be no rest till this race is complete,

as they race in the **waka ama**.

KIA TERE
GO KIDS. ROW
YOU CAN DO IT
KIA TERE
GO TEAM
KIA TERE
5
4
3
2
1

They can hear the crowd cheering them on:

"**Kia kaha, kia kaha, kia kaha** — be strong!"

"**Hoea! Hoea! Hoeaa!**" they call.

"**Kia tere! Kia tere! Kia tere** — give more!"

With a final huge effort from muscles that ache,

they edge past their rivals and make a quick break.

They cross the line at the end of the race —

by just a few seconds they've come in first place!

The teamwork of **waka ama**.

OME ON
KIA KAHA
KIA TERE
HOEA TŌ WAKA
KIA KAHA
HOEA
5
KIA TERE
4
3
2
HOEA
1

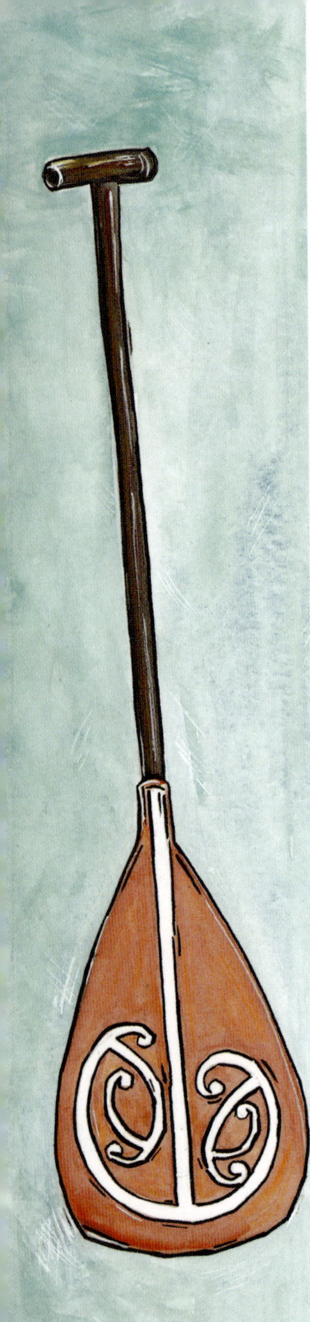

There are beaming smiles on the tired faces
of the boys who paddled so fast in their races.
Their muscles and backs ache from the strain
of paddling hard through sunshine and rain,
and making their paddles dip and row
to make the **waka** move fast and flow
across the sea, so calm and smooth
that rippled and glinted as it moved,
while the **kaihautū** chanted and watched the sea
and guided the **waka** to where it should be.
He'd led the boys so determined and strong
to work as a team and chant a song
while racing the **waka ama**.

4
5

As they left the shed beside the bay
that held the **waka** they'd paddled all day,
bathed in the light from the setting sun,
their day of paddling was nearly done.
They gathered together for a last **karakia**,
a prayer of thanks that they'd had no fear.
Then the boys all stretched and yawned —
it had been a very long day since dawn
of paddling the **waka ama**.

Tahi, rua, toru, whā,

hī!

Glossary

Hoe (ho eh) — to paddle, row

Hoea! Hoea! Hoeaa! (ho eh ah) — the paddling call, *Row! Row! Row!*

Hoea tō waka! (ho eh ah toe wa ka) — row your boat!

Kaihautū (ky hoe too) — lead paddler, sits at the back calling instructions

Kaihoe (ky ho eh) — paddlers

Karakia (ka ra kee ah) — prayer

Kia kaha! (kee ah ka ha) — be strong, keep going!

Kia tere! (kee ah teh reh) — faster!

Waka (wa ka) — canoe

Waka ama (wa ka ah ma) — outrigger canoe

Whānau (far no) — family